Wherever you are,
wherever I am,
at night we will
be looking at
the same sky.
Always,
Your loving
Mutti

SEEKING REFUGE

A GRAPHIC NOVEL

Published in Canada by Tradewind Books in 2016
Published in the USA and the UK by Tradewind Books in 2017

Based on *Remember Me* a novel by Irene N. Watts, published by Tundra Books 2000

Book design by Elisa Gutiérrez
The text of this book is set in Borrowdale, Grenale Slab and Halis Rounded.

10 9 8 7 6 5 4 3 2 1

Library and Archives Canada Cataloguing in Publication

Watts, Irene N., 1931-
[Remember me]
Seeking refuge / Irene N. Watts ; illustrations by Kathryn Shoemaker.

Adaptation of author's novel entitled Remember me.
ISBN 978-1-926890-02-9 (paperback)

1. World War, 1939-1945--Refugees--Comic books, strips, etc. 2. World War, 1939-1945--Refugees--Juvenile fiction. 3. Kindertransports (Rescue operations)--Comic books, strips, etc. 4. Kindertransports (Rescue operations)--Juvenile fiction. 5. Graphic novels. I. Shoemaker, Kathryn E., illustrator II. Title. III. Title: Remember me.

PN6733.W39S44 2016 j741.5'971 C2016-901025-2

Printed and bound in Canada on ancient forest-friendly paper.

The publisher thanks the Government of Canada and Canadian Heritage for their financial support through the Canada Council for the Arts, the Canada Book Fund and Livres Canada Books. The publisher also thanks the Government of the Province of British Columbia for the financial support it has given through the Book Publishing Tax Credit program and the British Columbia Arts Council.

Irene N. Watts

SEEKING REFUGE

A GRAPHIC NOVEL

illustrations by

Kathryn E. Shoemaker

TRADEWIND BOOKS
VANCOUVER • LONDON

For Julia Everett and in memory of A. J. Watts, 1927-2015

Thanks to the entire team at Tradewind Books.
Special thanks to Kathryn E. Shoemaker for once again
bringing Marianne to life—I.N.W.

• •

For Irene, thank you for another great story—K.E.S.

CONTENTS

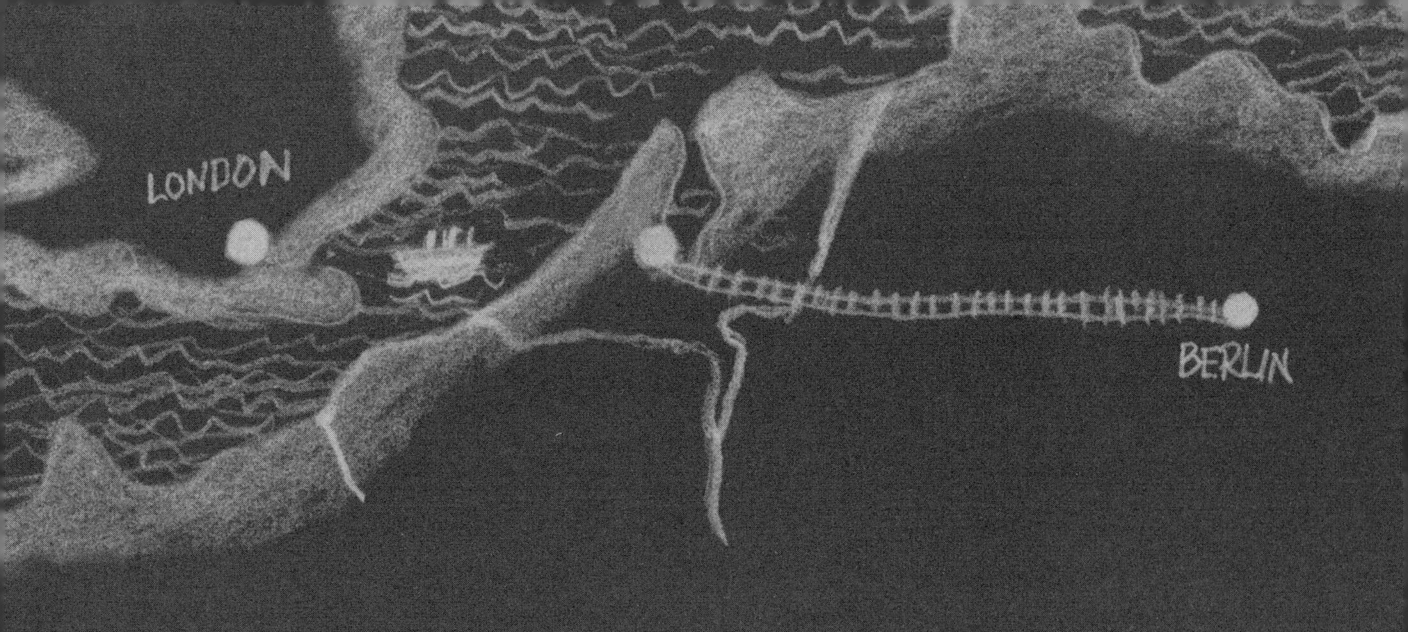

Chapter One • "Like Animals at the Zoo"

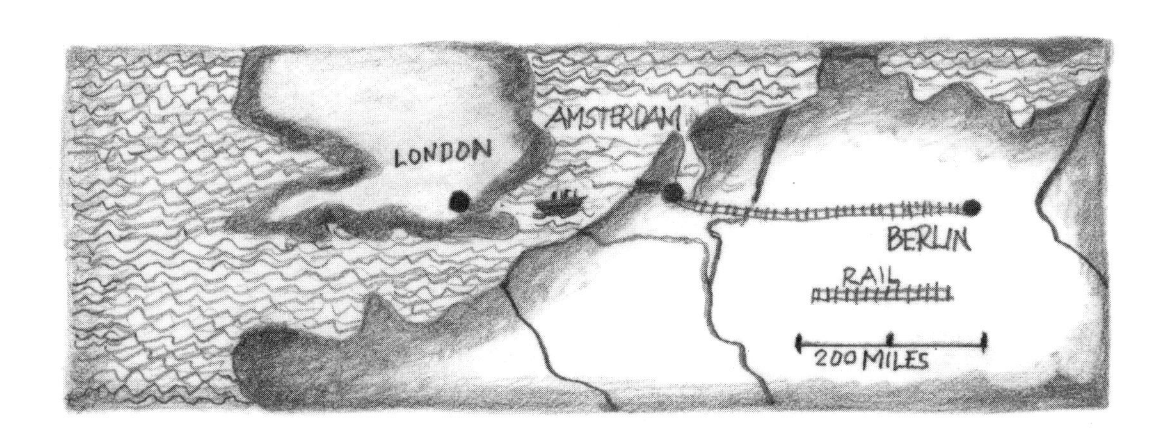
LONDON
AMSTERDAM
BERLIN
RAIL
200 MILES

London, England. December 2, 1938
Next stop: Liverpool Street Station. All change.
Stay close beside me, Sophie. Don't get lost.
Mind your backs.
Smile!

We'd better smile. Make a good impression.
Like animals at the zoo.

Look at me. Sophie, your face is dirty.

Are we going to our new families now?

Soon.

Twenty-four hours ago, I said good-bye to *Mutti* in Berlin. And now I'm in London!

Who's taking you in?
I don't know. I feel as if I've been travelling for a thousand years.

The Thousand-year Reich. The Nazis can't get us here.

I am Miss Baxter. Welcome. Please follow me.

More German refugees! Why bring them here?
Look at that little one. Sweet, isn't she?
See them poor little refugees.
Come on, Sophie. Keep up.

We must try to speak English all the time.
I don't know how. I want to go home!

Hurry up, Bernd. Father said stay together.
Look! A man gave me a penny. He said, "Here you are, son."
You can't speak English. And you're not supposed to talk to strangers.
We're all strangers. We don't know anyone, do we?

If she cries, I'll start too.
No, I suppose not.
Sorry, I only meant . . .

Come on, Sophie. Catch up! Isn't the lady wearing that red hat clever–like a bird showing the way?
Like Hansel and Gretel. Will everyone be nice in England?

Much nicer than in Germany. Nazis don't hold our hands.

Are you hungry?
Here you are, dear.
Sit down and wait until you hear your name called. Each sponsor will be paired with a child on my list. Numbers must match.

Reverend Smithe, and Peter and Annemarie Weiss.
Johann Fuchs and Mr. Green.

Is that your little sister sleeping?
No. Her mother asked me to look after her. Just until we got to England.

Waiting's horrible, isn't it?
Sophie Mandel and Miss Simmonds.
That's you, Sophie Wake up.

Hello, Sophie. I am Aunt Margaret. Your mother's friend. You are going to live with me.
Marianne?

She looks nice. Goodbye, Sophie.

I won't know anyone now.
Suppose no one comes for me. Why did I agree to go?
Dear Mutti
I'm in Liverpool Street
Station Please
write me
here

ONE, TWO, THREE.

Is your name Leah Stein?

Ich heisse Marianne . . . Sorry–my name is *Marianne* Kohn.

Your name isn't here. See Miss Martin. She speaks German.

An orphan got measles. I was offered her place.

Please no send back! Gestapo. I am Jewish.
Don't be afraid. You won't be sent back.
Are they whispering about me?

You are safe now. Why didn't you stay at the hostel with the other orphans when you arrived?
I am not an orphan. I just travelled with them.

I've put your name on my list. Now you're official!
Sank you.
I am Mrs. Abercrombie-Jones. Is this girl Leah Stein?

Stay where you are, *Marianne*.

Leah has not arrived, but *Marianne* is in need of a sponsor.
Who?
Marianne, pronounced as Marianna.

I expected an older girl as a domestic help. Not a child! Why wasn't I notified?

We didn't know. This is the first *Kindertransport* the Nazis allowed to leave Germany.

How old are you?

I am eleven and one half years old.

Do you speak English?

Yes, please. I speak a little.
I can say please, good-bye, and thank you. I brought Father's dictionary with me.

She looks young for her age. But as I've told everyone we are sponsoring a refugee, I'll have to take her.
SIGH
Very well. Come along, Mary Anne.

She doesn't seem very motherly. I hope we get to like each other.

Chapter Two • Welcome to London

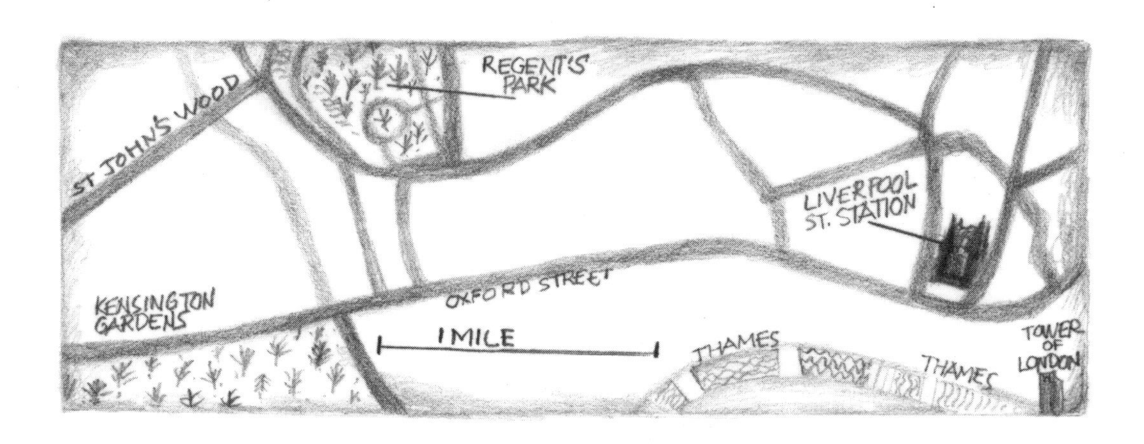
REGENT'S PARK
ST JOHN'S WOOD
LIVERPOOL ST. STATION
KENSINGTON GARDENS
OXFORD STREET
1 MILE
THAMES
THAMES
TOWER OF LONDON

Here I am in the biggest, most wonderful city in the whole world.
Watch where you're going, ducks.

I'm sorry, Constable. She's a refugee from Germany.

No harm done, ma'am. Welcome to London, miss.

Taxi!

My first taxi ride, *Mutti*.
Twelve Circus Road, St. John's Wood, please.

She lives in a circus? Grandfather told me a joke. I hear they're training seals to bark '*Heil* Hitler.'

Ahem...
More questions. I hope I understand.

I'm dying for my tea. Aren't you?
Yes, please.

Where did you learn to speak English, Mary Anne?
I learn in school.

I like werry much go to school.

Very much, not 'werry.'

School. She can start Monday. Out of my way.

I keep seeing Mutti's face, hearing her voice.

Fit in and be grateful. When you meet people, ask them to sponsor us for work in England.

'Ere you are, ma'am. 12 Circus Road.

It's not a circus.
Just a street.

Good afternoon, madam.

This is Mary Anne. And this is our maid, Gladys.

Welcome, miss.
She smiles as if she means it.
Tea in ten minutes, Gladys.

You can wash and unpack before tea.
She speaks too fast. Do I say "yes"?

This is the bathroom. Do you have running water at home?
Yes.

This is your room. Gladys sleeps next door. Come down when you're ready.
Sank you.

This is the loneliest place in the world.

I thought I'd look more English by now.

No need to stand there. Come in and say, "How do you do."
All those dishes! If the Gestapo came here, they'd smash them.

How do you do?
Mary Anne, This is Mr. Abercrombie-Jones and the Reverend James.

I have enjoyed walking in your beautiful country, *Marianne*.
He speaks German, and pronounces my name properly—he must be a spy.

Well done, Vicar. Do sit down.

I've never tasted tea with milk before.
Have some cake.

I can't swallow a bite. I'll just throw it in the fire.

You may help Gladys. Then come in and say goodnight.

I'll wash. You dry. Put the dishes on the table.

Good. Go and say good-night to madam, now.

I must be polite. Also I have to ask something.

KNOCK!
KNOCK!

I write my mother. Where this house, please?

London, England. I'll write the address down.
Also please, your name?

Mr. and Mrs. Abercrombie-Jones. Call me Uncle Geoffrey and my wife, Aunt Vera.
Onkel Geoffrey. Aunt Wera. In German, my name is *Marianne*.

Vera has a hard sound. Uncle Geoffrey's name is pronounced with a G. Do you understand?

Yes, please. Aunt Wera, I need stamp. I haf marks.

The stamp is a present.
Sank you. Goodnight.
Goodnight, Mary Anne.

MUMBLE
SIGH

It's cold.

Is it safe to write home? What if the Nazis find the letter?

Dear

CREAK!

Who is there? Is someone coming in to say goodnight?

Don't feel sad, Teddy. We'll get used to England. It will just take a while.

Chapter Three • **Lost**

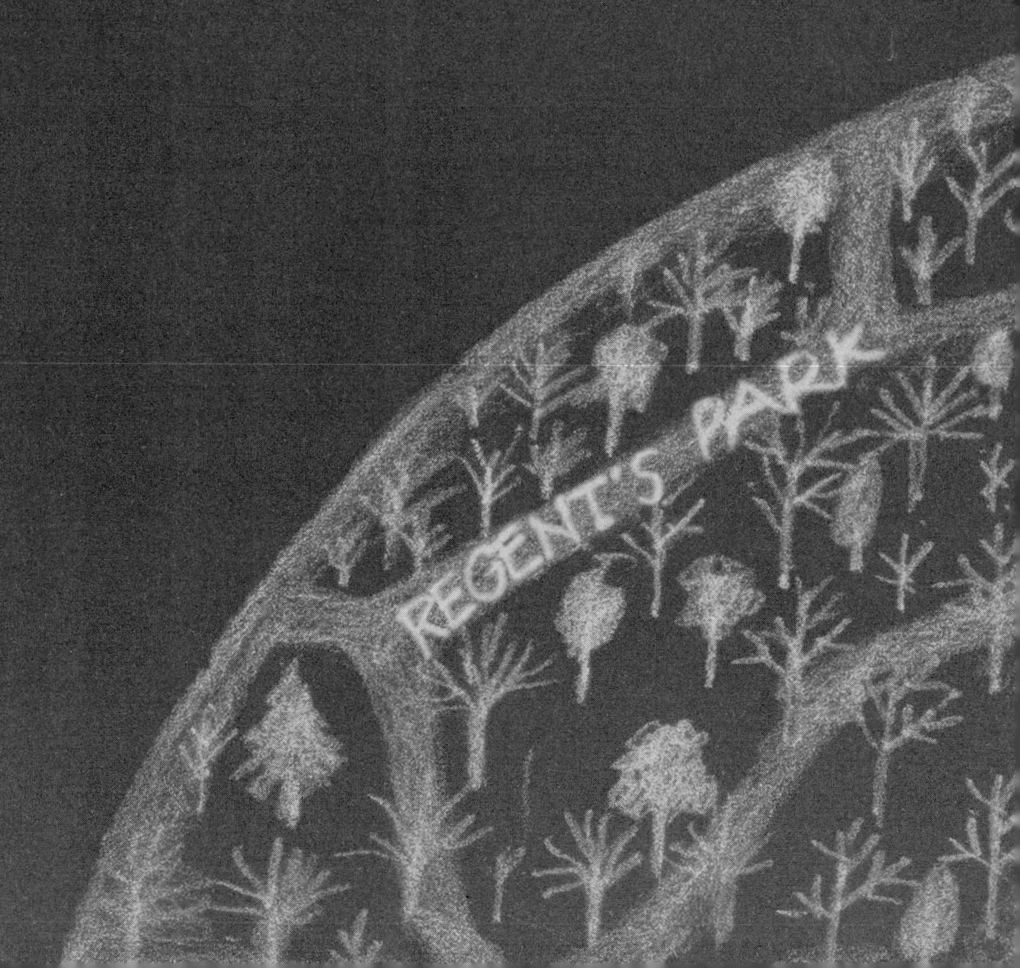

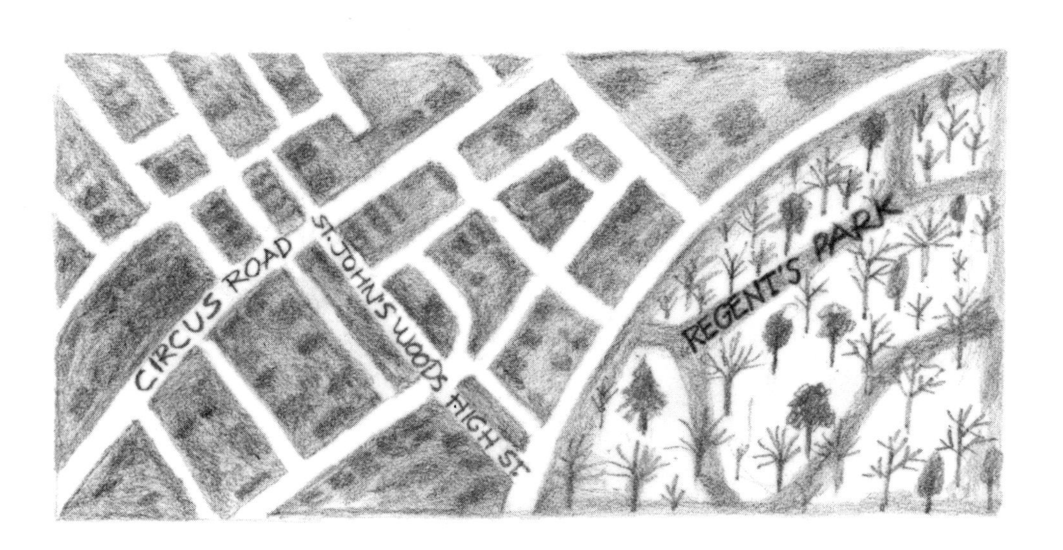
CIRCUS ROAD
ST. JOHN'S WOODS HIGH ST.
REGENT'S PARK

Here's your porridge.
I'm starved.

What is this horrible stuff?

I'll throw this down the sink.

At home, I'd be eating rolls and cherry jam.

I wish I'd said good-bye to *Vati* and *Oma* and *Opa*.
What language is that?

German. Sorry, I forgot.

Good morning, Mary Anne.
Good morning Aunt W-Wera.

Vera. Gladys, we are leaving now. Let Mary Anne help you.
Who is leaving? I don't understand.

You dust downstairs.

Come with me.

I'll just dust around the ornaments.

Well done! Go and make your bed.

12 Circus Road
St. John's Wood
London, NW8
England

3 December

Dear Mutti,

I arrived safely. I have
my own room. There is
plenty to eat. I speak
English. Aunt Vera says
I may start school next
Monday. I was happy
to find your letter!

Wherever you are,
Wherever I am,
at night we will
be looking at the
same sky.
Always
Your loving
Mutti

I'm fine.
Come soon.
Much love and
kisses from Marianne

I'll never tell Mutti how lonely I am.

Please, Gladys– where I post letter?
Turn left. The red pillarbox is around the corner. Put on your coat.

BOOKS
BOOKS

BOOK

Books
No!
Here too! *Vati* would say it is a free country with many books.

Be careful, dear.
She sounds like *Mutti*. I'll sit down. The bench doesn't say FOR ARYANS ONLY.

Good-bye, dear.

Is this the way I came in? It will get dark soon.

He's in uniform. I'm afraid to ask him.

Are you lost? Don't cry.

Go out by the North Gate. Turn left, then right, cross the High Street . . .
Please, I not understand.

Follow me.

You'll be alright now.

Here she is, Madam.
Where have you been? What will the neigh-bours think? Answer me!

Sorry, I lose the way.

You've missed tea. Go to your room.

No!
Did I scream?
It was only a bad dream. One more day before school starts.

Will I make friends?
How do you do?

MONDAY MORNIG
I'll tell Miss Barton you are here.

I can't stay.
I have an appointment. Be a good girl, Mary Anne. Good-bye.

You must be Mary Anne. Come and meet your class.

Be seated. This is a new student, Mary Anne Kohn, a refugee from Germany. Please make her welcome. Thank you.

Good morning, Miss Barton.

Mary Anne, you may sit over there.

Bridget, look after Mary Anne today.
Yes, sir.
They all seem very nice.

Herbert Brown, take a detention.
HUN
I'll help you. Starting a new school is awful!

Arctic
Chilly
Blizzard
Icicle
Glacial
numb
Snowdrifts
Use each word in a sentence.

I brought you some cocoa, to warm you up.
Sank you, Gladys. You kind person. I finish homework. Goodnight.

Aunt Vera's face is glacial when she looks at me.

Goodnight, *Mutti.*

Chapter Four • Refugee

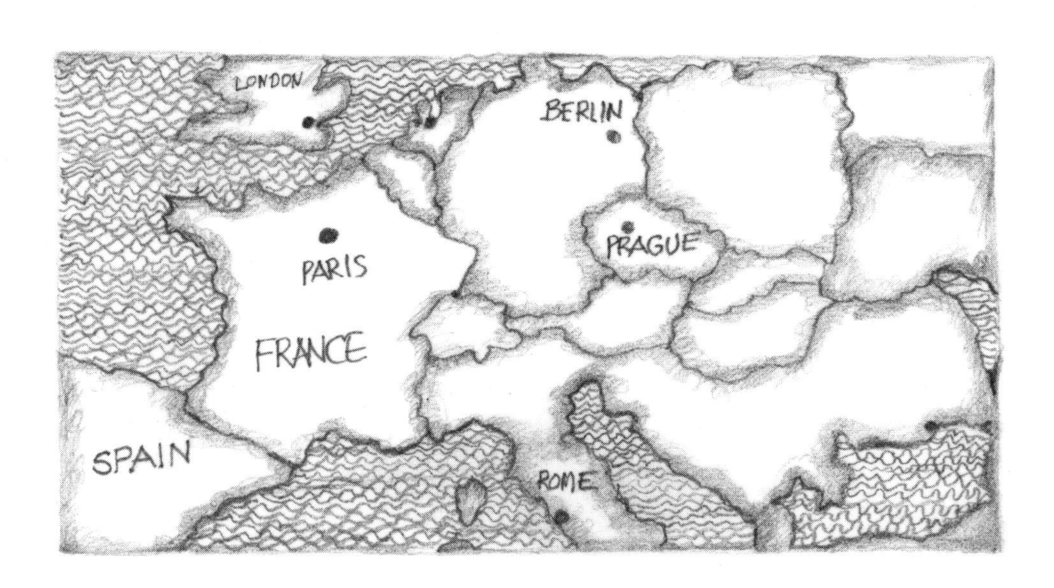
LONDON
BERLIN
PARIS
PRAGUE
FRANCE
SPAIN
ROME

Today is my bridge afternoon. You may help serve tea to my friends.
Yes, Aunt W-Vera.
I'll ask the English ladies for help.

Don't they ever stop talking?

What a becoming frock, Phoebe!
My new dressmaker, a refugee from Vienna, made it.
My mother sews. Is werry good cook. Father speaks English. You have work? Here is address to write, please.

Give me that paper! Fresh tea, Mary Anne. And stay in the kitchen!
A foreigner? Our cook would not approve.
Don't be cross, Vera. How sweet and brave to ask!

Madam wants to see you after the ladies leave.

Naturally you miss your parents. That is no excuse to embarrass me.
Is it wrong to help my parents?

They must wait their turn. A refugee needs good manners.
I hate this word "refugee."

I am waiting for an apology.
Never behave like this again in my house. And stop biting your nails. It is an ugly habit! That's all.
Sorry.

DOOR BELL: DING, DONG!
STUMP, STUMP

KNOCK!
KNOCK!
Ready for your English lesson? I've brought Pa's *Times* so you can practice reading aloud.

I have an idea! Don't tell Aunt Wera.
Vera, like vampire. I promise.

To get visa my parents need work. I knock on doors, ask. Help me what to say, please?
That's brilliant!

Sank you.
Put your tongue between your teeth. Try again.

Thank you. Is better?
Much. Look in the *Times* under "Domestic Situations Required."

Here is one from Berlin! "I am girl of eighteen. I like dress-making. Am fond of children."
I can easily change the words a bit. I'll borrow Pa's typewriter. We'll start on Saturday.

Madam says you are giving her a migraine.
Please tell her sorry.

Listen. "Gifted Jewish dressmaker . . ."

Say "Good cook. Likes children."
Gifted Jewish
dressmaker, good
cook, likes children
seeks domestic
England.
as gardener
man
What does your father do?
He sold books once, before . . .

"Husband works as gardener/ handyman." Write down the address for replies.

We've finished our English lesson, Mrs. Abercrombie-Jones. Mother sends her regards.
Thank you, dear. Give her mine, too.

A well brought-up child. Go and help Gladys serve now.
Yes, Aunt Wera. Vera.

Do you think she does it on purpose, Geoffrey?

A Few Days Later

Come round the back to the tradesmen's entrance. I'll ring the bell first.
No, I must. It's for my parents.

There's no one about. Push the note under the door. My turn!

I will make sure this gets delivered, young ladies.

Let's try one more.
NO HAWKERS

Little girls, you vant help? Come back.
Sank you.

It is cold. I am *Miriam Levy*. I am maid.

I'm *Marianne* Kohn from Berlin. I'm looking for work for my parents, so they'll get visas.

I'm trying to bring my mother here. My father and brother are in a concentration camp.
My father was in one, but he got away. I don't know where he is.

COUGH

Bridget, Miriam is a refugee like me! Miriam, this is my best friend, Bridget. She helps me.
I am pleased to meet you.

DING, DONG!
Madam is home from shopping. I must go. If I hear of something, I write.
Thank you. Good-bye.

Thanks for coming with me, Bridget.
It's nothing. First one to step on a crack is out!
I haven't heard your name pronounced like that before. *Marianna*. It sounds nice.

If I don't step on a crack, my parents will get their visas!

This came for you today.

That's funny. I don't know anyone living there.

Hello Marianne,
Prague is a beautiful city
with many books.
I think of you often.
Love to you and your
mother.
D.

D for David, father's name. He's being awfully secretive. There's no address. Why? The Nazis aren't in Prague!
He's safe. He's safe. Dancing keeps me warm. It's freezing up here.

Are you warm and safe from the Gestapo now?
Mary Anne, come downstairs please.

I see someone sent you a card from Prague. Do you have friends there?
My father.

Is he on holiday?

Beautiful city. Bridges, statues. Our glass decanter was made there.

Holiday? Don't they understand what's going on? *Vati* had to escape across the frontier.

Stop dreaming. Answer my question.

No, not holiday. He runs from Hitler. like me.

You exaggerate, Mary Anne. Goodnight.

I've outgrown my shoes. I'll look for a second-hand pair at the school jumble sale tomorrow.

SALE IN AID OF SPANISH WAR REFUGEES
BOOKS

Bridget would love *Swallows and Amazons* for her birthday!
How much is this book, please?

Twopence. Good choice!

What are you looking for?
Walking shoes, size three and a half.

There's a box of shoes under the table.
How much for this pair, please?
SHOES

They're like new. I'll let them go for nine pence.
I only have four pence with me.
May I be of help?

Everyone will know I need shoes.
I didn't bring enough money, sir.

Would a loan help?
Thank you, sir. I can repay you on Monday.

I was saving up for more stamps, but I can't go barefoot.

Where did you get those shoes?
I bought them at the jumble sale.

Where did you get the money?
I had some. Mr. Neame lent me the rest. My feet grow too big.

You have shamed me in front of everyone.

I am werry sorry, Aunt Vera. You send me away?

This once, I will overlook your behaviour. What can one expect from a refugee?
SIGH

Why does she hate me?

Come soon, *Mutti.*

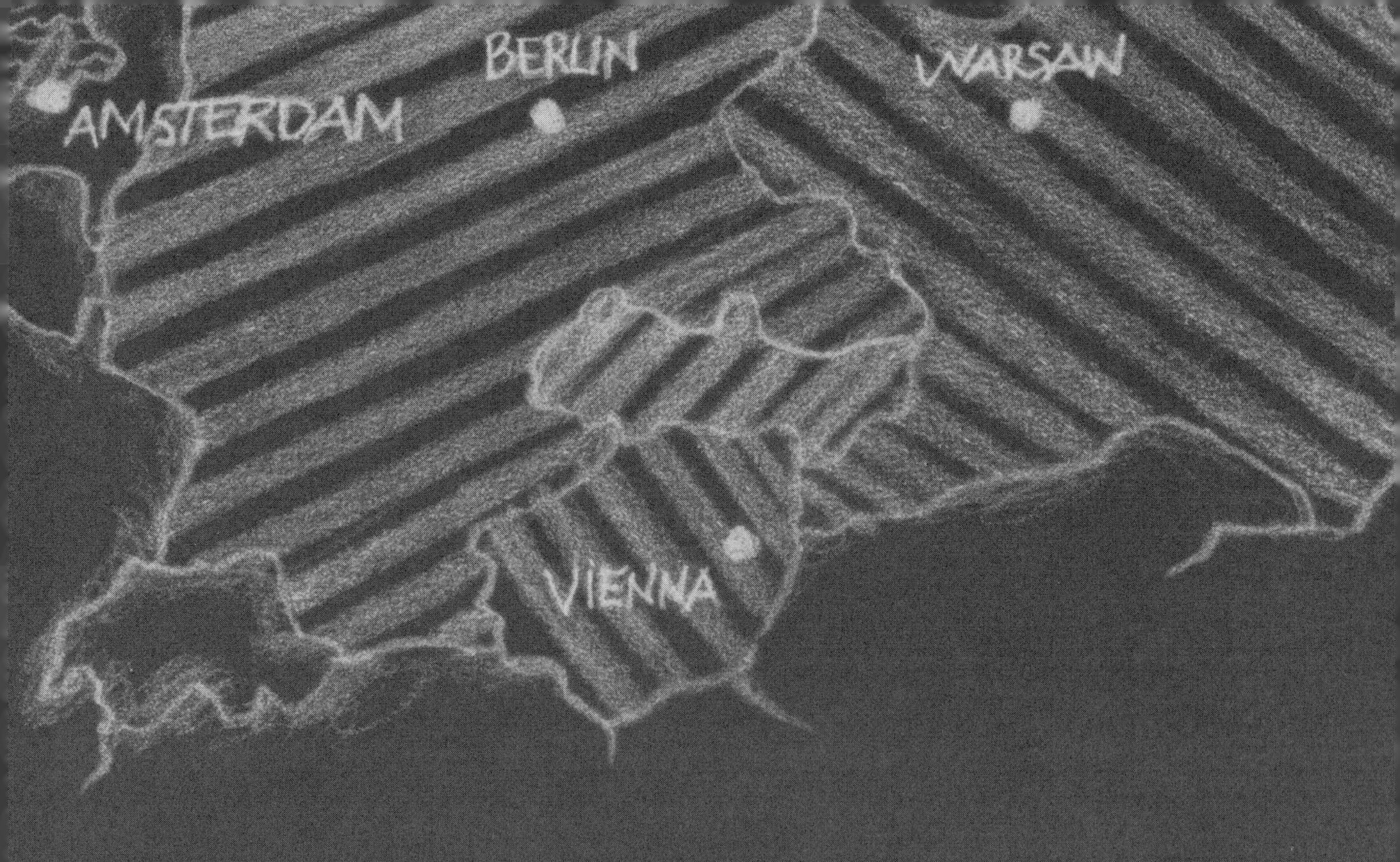

Chapter Five • Waiting for War

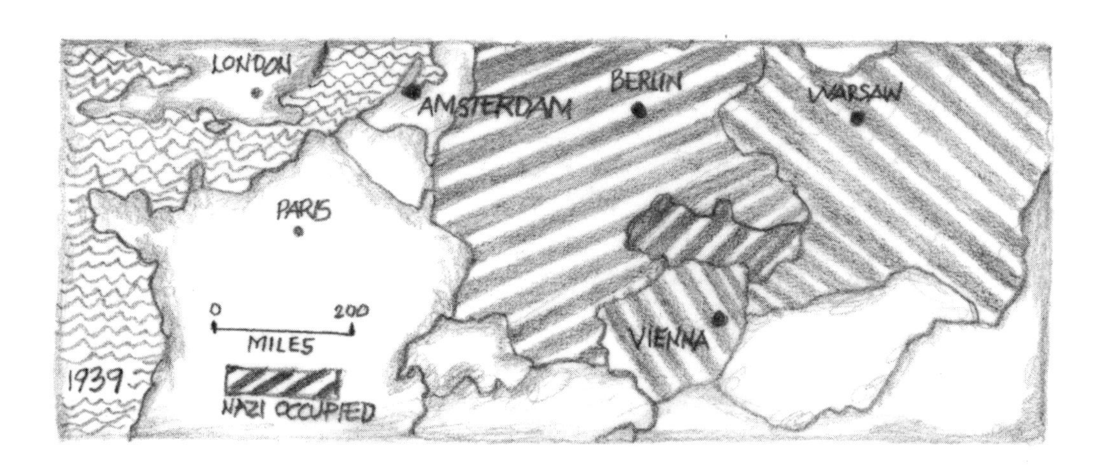
LONDON
AMSTERDAM
BERLIN
WARSAW
PARIS
0
200
MILES
VIENNA
1939
NAZI OCCUPIED

They just let them walk in! Foreigners–no backbone!
Where will *Vati* hide now?
NAZI TROOPS
MARCH IN PRAGUE

If Aunt Vera finds me walking in my sleep, I'll be in trouble.
Our advertisements will work. Don't worry.

I can't help it! Father can't get out. The Nazis have invaded Czechoslovakia.
I'll change the "gardener/ handyman" bit. Sorry.

As the months pass, Britain prepares for war.
Those barrage balloons remind me of fat Marshall Goering. He'll bomb us.
We'll be at war soon. Isn't it exciting?

Pa says the balloons will confuse the enemy planes and they'll go back home.
If there's no danger, why build shelters?

I hate gas mask drills. The smell of rubber makes me feel sick.
I hate the way my ears roar inside the mask.

Hold your breath, girls. Chins out. Grasp the straps. Pull them over your head, and don't take the masks off until I whistle.
Why haven't I heard from *Mutti*?
Only two weeks before the summer holidays. Will we be at war?

You may have to leave the masks on for much longer, if the enemy drop gas bombs!

Have I got a letter?
Yes.

June 2, 1939

Dear Marianne

Two weeks ago I heard from a lady in England who needs a housekeeper. It will not be easy to leave your grandparents to manage alone. Jews may shop only one hour a day and Oma and Opa must leave their home. But we agreed that when my exit permit arrives I should come to England.

Love from all of us

Mutti

THE GOVERNMENT SENDS PAMPHLETS TO ALL HOMES IN BRITAIN.
How to be safe
Alway carry your gas mas
What to do in an airraid if the invad
How to Gas

Even a sliver of light makes us a target.

I do not intend to run short of food under siege!

Hitler's taken over Vienna and Prague! Will London be next?

The summer holidays begin.
It's too hot to start a war! Let's go for a swim tomorrow.
Last time I went swimming in Berlin . . .

JEWS AND DOGS NOT ADMITTED

I don't have a bathing suit.
I'll lend you one. See you in the morning!

I'm catching the train to Torquay. Mr. Abercrombie-Jone's office is relocating. We must find a flat.
On my day off, Madam? I had plans.
It's not like Gladys to be in a bad mood.

We all must make sacrifices. Listen to radio announcements.
Do you mean about trains, Aunt Vera?

Don't be impertinent. War is imminent. Clean your room and polish the floor.

Why would invaders care about my floor?
KNOCK!

Come outside, Marianne.

I'm sorry I can't go swimming.
What's happened?

I'm being evacuated.
I know that. We're all going! But not yet.

They're sending me to Canada, to live with relatives.
Do you have to go?

I begged my parents to let me stay. Pa said, "You'll be safer there."
They always say that! When do you leave?

The boat sails tomorrow. Here's my new address.

We'll stay friends forever!

It's come! Evacuation starts tomorrow. You have to be at school by 6:30 am.

Madam rang up. She can't get back in time. She said I'm to give you half a crown.

Thank you, Gladys. I'll go and pack.

Aunt Vera never wanted me.

1st. Septem 1939
Dear Aunt Vera and Uncle Geoffrey,
Thank you for taking me in and for the half crowns, I am grateful.
Yours sincerely,
Marianna Kohn

Good luck, Mary Anne. I made you lunch to eat on the train.
Good-bye, Gladys. Thank you for everything.

Off to the country? My lad's going too. Got a card for you. Good luck!

Good-bye.
Thank you so much.

Dear Marianne
I love you.
Remember me.
Vati

Chapter Six • Evacuation

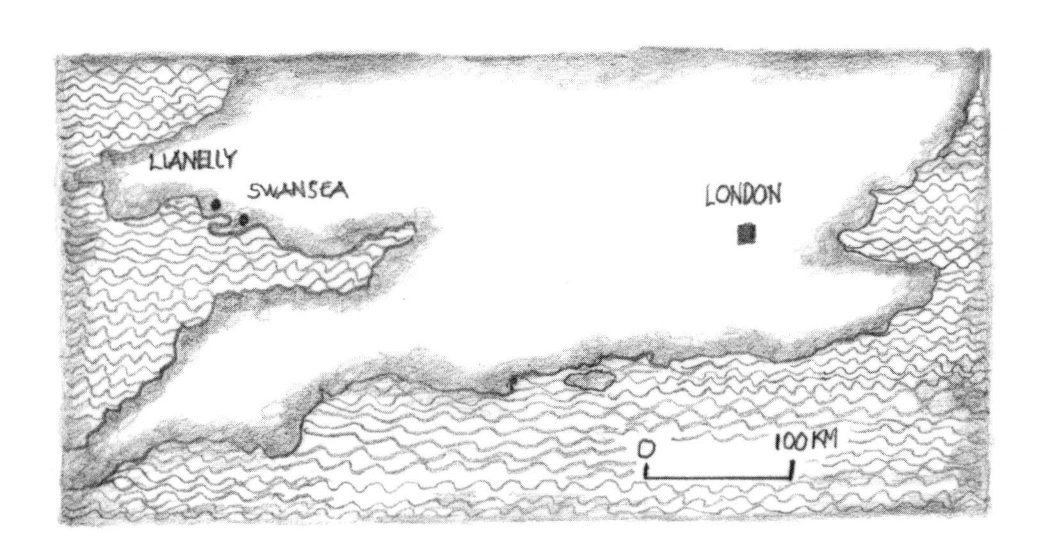

LLANELLY
SWANSEA
LONDON
0
100 KM

On the 1st of September, 1939, three million children leave the cities of Britain for the safety of the countryside. All rail travel is reserved for the evacuation.
Print your name and your school. You must wear these labels until we arrive.
We won't forget our names, Miss Barry.

In the event of an accident, it will help to identify you.
It's like the *Kinder-transport* all over again!

RING!
The buses are here to take us to the station. Don't forget your gas masks.

GOODBYE
HITLER

Look after your sister.
Stay together.
I'm the only one without someone to see me off.
Write us the minute you get there.

Barley sugar–the best remedy for travel sickness!
I wish I'd stayed in London.
When will we get there?

I have no idea, but prepare for a long journey.
I'm just down the corridor, two compartments along, if you need me. This will be a great adventure.

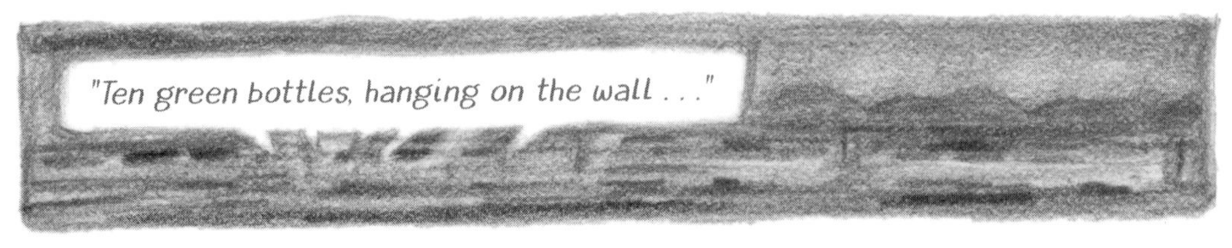
"Ten green bottles, hanging on the wall . . ."

"Daisy, Daisy, give me your answer do."
"It's a long way to Tipperary . . ."

Llanelly is a friendly town. Dusty, coal all around us, slag heaps like mountains. There's everything you need: church, chapel, cinema, and a rugby team.

Old Road School. Half the town's there, getting ready for you. Even the Mayor.
Where are we going?

WELCOME
We are most pleased to welcome you to Wales.

THE YOUNGEST AND PRETTIEST CHILDREN ARE THE MOST SOUGHT AFTER AND ARE QUICKLY TAKEN.

Aros–wait. Sign your name, address, and your foster child's name. We don't want to lose anyone.

How old are you, dear?
I'm twelve.

And where are you from, *bach*?
Mary Anne is a Jewish refugee from Germany.

Oh? No, thanks. I don't think so.

WELCOME

Is it because I wear glasses?
Bridget wears glasses. They suit you, Lucy. I know what's wrong with me.

There's nothing wrong with either of you.

We weren't expecting so many evacuees.
Dorothy and Jenny, I'll take you to the nurse's hostel. Lucy and Mary Anne, follow Mr. Evans.

We don't have far to go.

Sospan fach yn berwiar y ta.
Is that Welsh?
Yes. *Sospan Fach* is the theme of the Scarlets rugby team.

What does it mean?
It is a silly song about a saucepan on a stove and a little cat who knocks it over.

Shwmae heno, Matron. How are you? Good of you to take Mary Anne and Lucy.
Come in. You'll have a cup of tea, Mr. Evans?

If it's no trouble.
I'll just show the girls upstairs.

Lucy, go in this room—and Mary Anne in here. Unpack and then come down.

I wish we were in the same room.
I'll see you in ten minutes.

How far are you gone?
Hello, I'm *Marianne* Kohn, an evacuee from London.

Pardon?

Ha ha ha!
Ha ha ha ha!

Please, where is the lavatory?

No fancy London ways. The running water comes from the sky. *Tŷ bach*—the little house—is outside.

Where are we?

This is the Methodist home for unmarried girls.

Come to the wrong place, have you?

Wait for me. I don't know what Miss Barry would say if she knew.

Sit down.

Before grace? Where do you come from?

For what we are about to receive, may the Lord make us truly thankful. Amen.
Amen.

Eat. When you're finished, wash your bowls in the scullery.

The privy's at the end of the path. Wash at the pump when you get back.

Wait for me. I'm terrified of spiders.

Make your beds before you come down. Breakfast is at seven.

If Miss Barry doesn't fetch us tomorrow, I shall catch the first train back to London!
Sleep well, Lucy. Goodnight.

Leave my things alone!

Are you calling me a thief?

Give that back to me! It's from my mother in Germany.
She's a spy, Dilys!

I'm too young to be a spy! I'm here to escape Hitler. I'm Jewish.

A Jew!

A Jew.

What is going on here?
She's a Jew, Matron.
A German spy!

I want my letter!

Into bed, girls. You, miss, come with me.

Wait here. Don't move until I come back.

Dirty spy!
Christ killer!

I am sorry, *bach.* A poor start indeed!

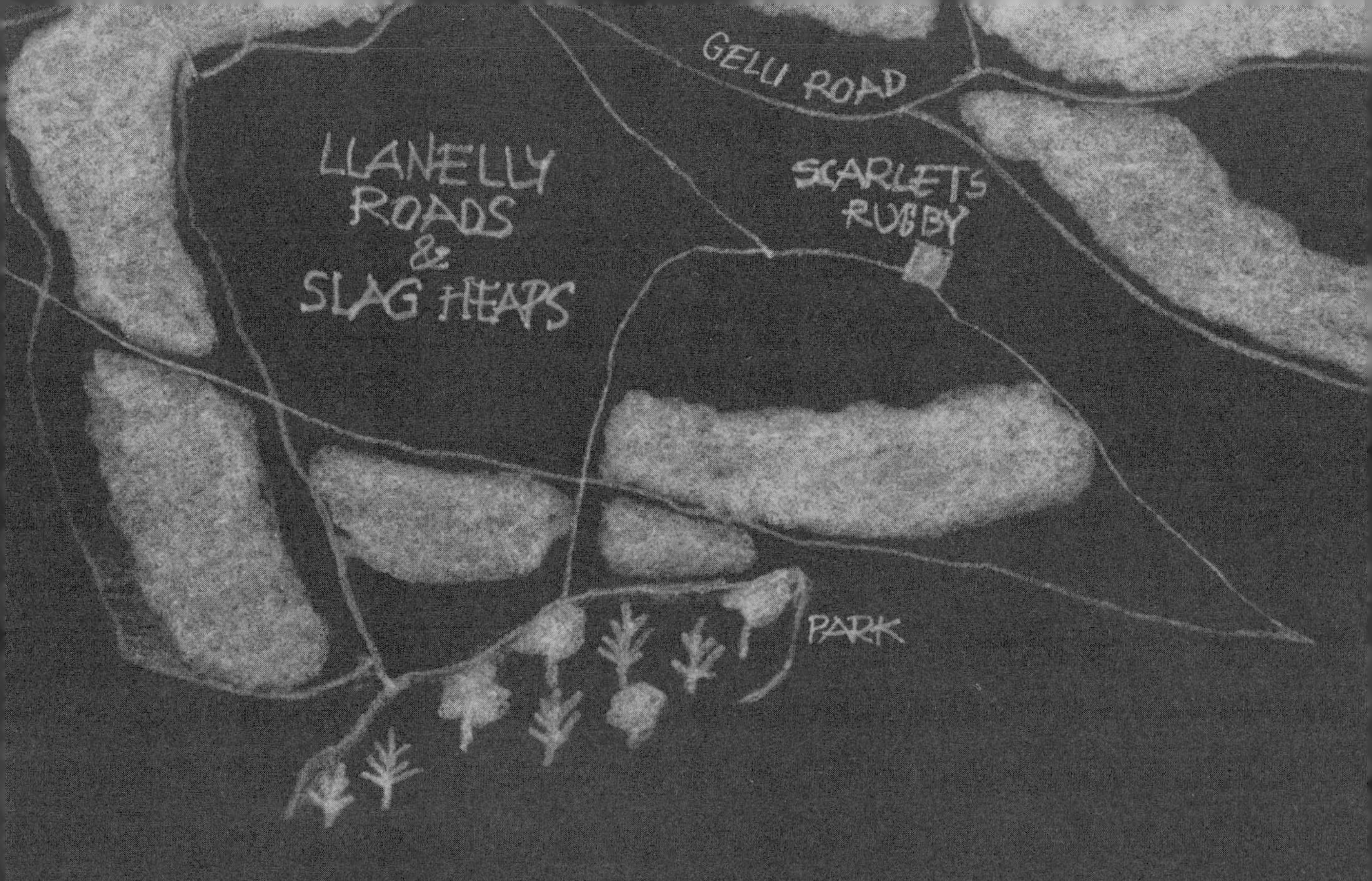

Chapter Seven • **Billets**

PWLL ROAD
BEACH
GELLI ROAD
LLANELLY
ROADS
&
SLAG HEAPS
SCARLETS
RUGBY
BEACH
LLANELLY
BEACH & TOWN
0
1
MILE
PARK

Y ferch Mam—the little girl. My mother has little English. I'll be back in the morning. *Nos da, Mam*—Goodnight, Mary Anne.

She's like a witch in a fairy story.

Thank you.
Dech y gwely—Come to bed.

It's kind of her to share her bed with a stranger.

Morning.

Bore da–good morning.

Good–no spiders!

Bara menyn–bread and butter.

Your house is beautiful.
Diolch–Thank you.

I'm glad I didn't see the cat last night!
KNOCK!

If I could stay here, I'd soon speak Welsh!
Bore da–good morning, *Mam*, Mary Anne.

Well now, *bach*.
Please Mr. Evans, wasn't Bach a composer?

He was. *Bach* in Welsh means "little" or "dear." Are you ready? I have found a nice billet for you.

Diolch, Mrs. Evans.
You sound a proper Welsh girl. Goodbye, *Mam*.

Is this a temporary billet, too?
Indeed no! Permanent, I hope.

66 QUEEN VICTORIA

Is this my new little girl? How skinny she is!

And how is your dear mother?

Doing well for eighty. She's taken a fancy to your little Mary Anne. Wants to keep her!

We'll take good care of her, Mr. Evans.
Diolch, Mr. Evans.
I'd better be off. More billets to find! Good-bye, ladies.

You can call me Auntie Vi. Soon you'll be calling me *Mam*.
Doesn't she know I have a mother?

I'll show you round. This is the front room. We use it on special occasions.

We had Elisabeth's funeral tea in here. That's her picture.
She was only ten.

I'm twelve.
Never mind. Come upstairs.

Put your clothes in the wardrobe, next to Elisabeth's dresses; perfect for two little sisters sharing.

You won't touch the doll, will you? Elisabeth was holding her doll as she died. Every day I think about her. You can dust your little sister's room, keep it nice.
I'm starting a headache.

Thank you, Auntie Vi.

It's hot and stuffy in here.

AAAH!

What is it? Have you a pain?

I'm fine, but I felt something touch my hand.

Beautiful, isn't it? Plenty of room for your nightdress too.

Don't want you getting a chill.
But it's summer.

I'm home.
That's your Uncle *Dai*, longing to meet his new little girl. He's on the railway-split shift on Saturdays. Be quick!

I'll soon be at school.

Here she is–an answer to our prayers!
Let me have a look at you.

How do you do, sir?

Uncle *Dai*, *Mairi*.
In German, my name is pronounced *Marianne*.

Mairi in Welsh. A pretty name for a nice little girl–right, *Mam*?
Yes, *Dai*.

Are other girls changing names too?

Eat your broth, *Mairi*. It was Elisabeth's favourite!
I'm beginning to dread the sound of her name!

Church or chapel, *Mairi*?
At home in Berlin, we used to go to–
This is your home now, *Mairi*. We go to chapel–Auntie sings in the choir. I'm off to work. Bye, both.

Shall I do the washing up, Auntie Vi?
No, no, go and play outside. Take Elisabeth's ball. Don't lose it.

I hope she's not going to watch me all the time!

Charlie Chaplin went to France, to teach the ladies how to dance. And this is what he taught them— heel, toe, over we go.

It's too hot to play. I wonder what Elisabeth died of?

May I go for a walk, Auntie, just to the library?
Wear your blazer, and don't be long.

Another London evacuee fond of reading! Ask your auntie to sign here. Then you may have your own library card.
Thank you.

Mary Anne! Sorry about last night. I was too afraid to leave my room.
It doesn't matter. Are you still there?

No, a teacher came early to take me away.
What's it like?

I share a bedroom with the boys, three-year-old twins. Uncle Tom's a miner. He keeps a pig in the coal shed. Is your billet nice?

Yes, but Auntie Vi worries. I'd better get back.

I'm shopping for Auntie Ethel. See you at school!

Your tea's ready.

How long before bedtime? I'll have to sleep in Elisabeth's bed!
Nos da, Elisabeth.
I know you're out there somewhere, *Mutti*. Please come and get me soon.

Chapter Eight • A New Name

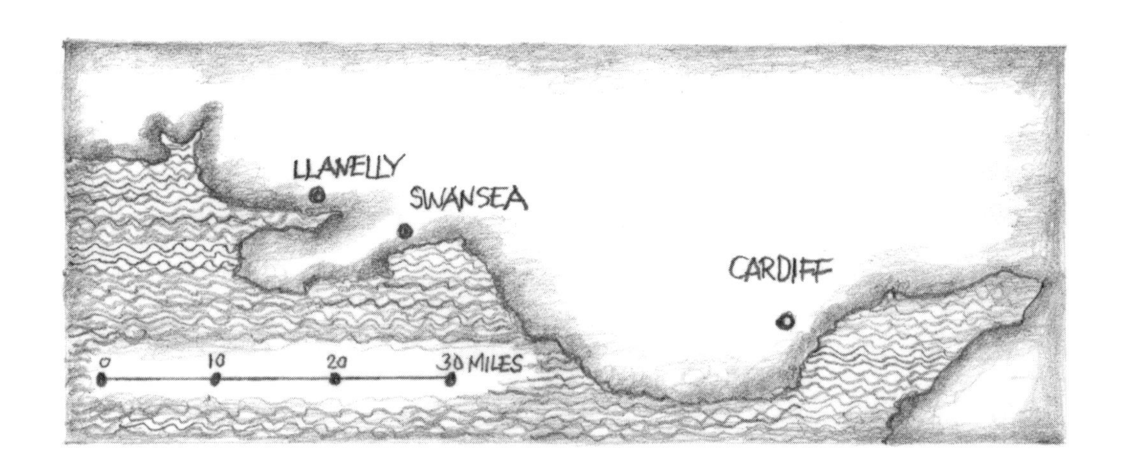
LLANELLY
SWANSEA
CARDIFF
0
10
20
30 MILES

You may wear Elisabeth's Sunday ribbon to go to chapel.
GREATER LOVE HATH NO MAN THAN HE LAY DOWN HIS LIFE FOR HIS FRIENDS
EEEOOOEEEOOO!
No chance of dozing off here!
FOR HIS FRIE
It is war. Let us pray for a conclusion to the evil that fills the world. There's the all-clear siren.
The French will never let the Germans through!
My boy's joining up tomorrow.
It won't be as bad as the last war!

Will the Nazis be dropped on the beach?
No, *bach*. The barbed wire will stop them!

How can *Mutti* come now?
Mairi, come down here.

I wish they'd call me by my real name!

This is Mrs. Jenkins, from next door.
Shwmae, *Mairi*. Call me Auntie *Blodwen*.
Shwame, Auntie *Blodwen*. I have to write a letter.

Sinful to write on a Sunday!
And to declare war! They should have waited.

I'll make a pot of tea.
Where are you from, *Mairi*? You don't sound like a Londoner.
I lived in Germany till last year.

Oh! So you speak German? Know Hitler, do you?
I don't speak German any more, Auntie *Blodwen*. Jews kept away from Hitler.

A Jew, never!

Have a Welsh cake, *Blodwen*.
I can't stay. Company coming for supper. Look at the time! Goodbye.
I shouldn't have said anything.

Funny, *Blodwen* going off like that!
May I go out for a walk, Auntie?

Don't forget your gas mask, and be home in thirty minutes.

SLAM!
It's all starting again.

28 September 1939

Dear Bridget,

I got your letter. Thanks. I'm glad you like living in Montreal. Auntie Vi wants to be my mother. She prays over me at night. I pretend to be asleep.

Last week, the school found lice in Hilary Brown's hair. She was in hysterics. We were all sent home to wash our hair with smelly black soap.

Blodwen Jenkins called me dirty MOCHYN when I passed her door. It means pig. You'd think I personally brought lice into Wales.

There's no news of the family yet.

Love from Marianne, also known as Mary Anne and also, Mairi.

My teacher is starting a rambling club this Saturday. Please may I go?
I had planned to take you to meet my sister. Your Auntie wants to meet her new niece!

Niece! We're not related!

As it's educational, you may go. Come home right after the walk is over, *Mairi*.
I will. Thank you.

Miss Ethel, with whom I'm billeted, gave me a recipe for Welsh cakes.
Mmm! Delicious, Miss Barry!
I never thought about teachers being billeted.

We're the same as you. And we feel homesick.
I dread Sundays– nothing but chapel!
They watch every bite I eat!
My foster mother reads my letters.
I have to use the dirty bath water after my foster sister!

The war is unlikely to be finished by Christmas.
I won't stay here for Christmas. I want my own room. I want my parents!
Look at that plane! There's been no air-raid warning. It must be one of ours.
Don't you mean theirs?
Shut up, Hilary!
She's always hinting I'm on the enemy side!
It looks like rain. Time to go.
Come and see our pig, Mary Anne.
All right, but I can't stay long.

COUGH! WHEEZE.
Who's that?
Auntie Ethel's father. His lungs are full of coal dust, from working down the mine.

That's Horace.

He doesn't have much room, does he?
We're fattening him up for Christmas. He gets our scraps.

I mustn't get too fond of him, because we'll eat him. Bacon and roast pork, trotters, chops, knuckles, and ears.

Ears? Are you. teasing me?
No. Mrs. Taylor singes off the hair and boils them, and they're fried up with onions.

What's wrong?
I feel sick.

At home with my parents, we don't eat pig.
Horace is my personal war effort. Every bit of food I can find is for him. See you Monday.

There's late you are, *Mairi*. It's Uncle *Dai's* dart night. Pork chops for supper.

I'm not hungry, Auntie Vi.
Be grateful for what the Lord provides *Mairi*. Sit down.

Eat up.
I can't. There's blood on my meat!

Got a chill, staying out in all weathers? No more rambles for you, *bach!*

After supper, we'll listen to the wireless. You can soak in the tub by the fire.

Time to go. *Nos da*, ladies.

Thank you, Auntie Vi. You are so kind to me.
Only Christian, isn't it? You're our little girl.

Chapter Nine • "*Mam* means Mother"

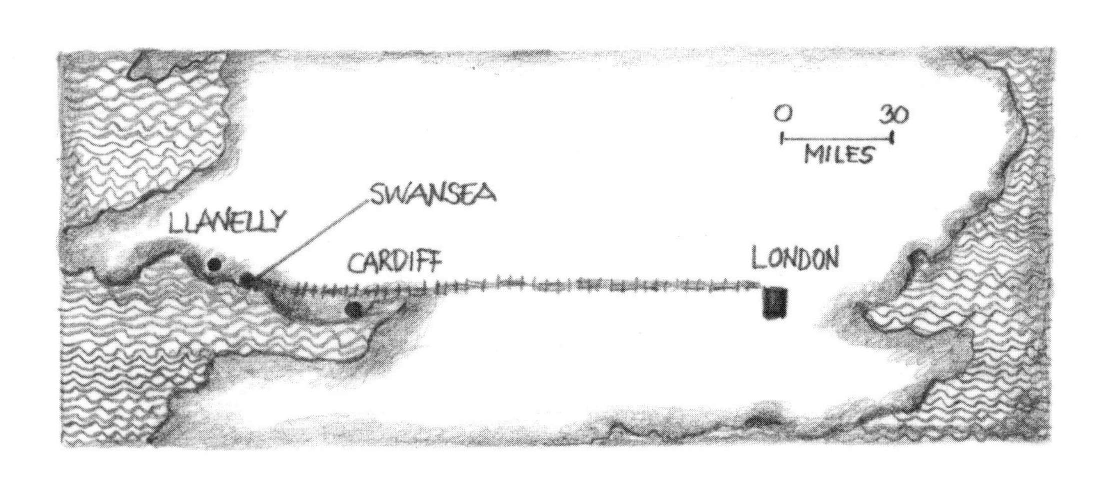

0
30
MILES
SWANSEA
LLANELLY
CARDIFF
LONDON

All our soldier boys will have new socks and warm scarves for Christmas.
Yes, Auntie Vi.

Call me *Mam, bach.*
But *Mam* means mother!

Yes, you're my proper little girl now—like Elisabeth.
I have a mother, Auntie Vi. I told you!

I never heard of a real mother sending her child away! *Mam* it is.
She sent me away because she loves me.

Nos da, Elisabeth.
What shall I do?
Mary Anne Kohn, where is your homework?
I'm sorry. It's at home. May I fetch it at recess?
You are spoilt and lazy, taking advantage, like the rest of your kind.
I don't understand what you mean by taking advantage, Miss Joyce.

Leave the room and stand in the corridor!

They'll probably expel me, and then I'll have to spend every moment with Auntie Vi!
Mary Anne? I never expected to see you here.

Good morning, Miss Lacey.

Come along to my office.

Sit down. How are you getting on in your billet?
Auntie Vi's changed my name. She wants me to call her 'Mother' and turn me into her dead child.

I have a mother.

Why didn't you tell me this before?
I didn't want to be a nuisance.

I am sure Mr. Evans and I can find the right billet for you.

Why were you sent out of class?
I forgot my homework and I answered back.

You may fetch your homework at recess.

Mary Anne, never give up hope.

THREE DAYS LATER
Mary Anne, you are going to a new billet today. Go straight home to pack.
It's only three days since I talked to Miss Lacey.
You're being moved. "Harbouring the enemy," *Blodwen* Jenkins said. Telling tales at that posh school, were you, Mary Anne?

I've put Elisabeth's room straight–the way it was before. To think you were going to be my own little girl!
I'm very sorry, Auntie Vi, Uncle *Dai*–but I belong to someone else.

Out of my house, wicked, ungrateful girl!

Hurry up, *bach*. Get in. There's cold it is for November.

I'm sorry to be a nuisance.
You are not, *bach*.

Out you get. Don't forget your case.

Where am I going?

To the Ladies' Waiting Room. I won't be long.

LADIES WAITING ROOM

Excuse me, please. I was told to wait here.

Mutti, is it you? Is it really you?
Marianne, you've got so tall!
I knew you'd come and find me!
The smoke's making my eyes water.
Mine too.
Train to London's due in five minutes.

Mr. Evans, how did you find her?
No one knew. Your *mam* surprised us. I'm happy for you both.
Thank you.
Diolch yn fawr, Mr. Evans.
I brought some sandwiches. You must be hungry.

Tell me every detail. How you got to England. How you found me.

Eat first. We have plenty of time now.
CARRY YOUR GAS MASK

WALLS HAVE EARS
ALWAYS CARRY YOUR GAS MASK

CARELESS TALK COSTS

It's safe to speak, *Mutti*.

Oma and *Opa* send their love.

I'd almost given up hope! Then my visa was stamped August 31st. I arrived in London on Saturday, September 2nd.

The day before war was declared. I was in Wales.

The house at 12 Circus Road was empty.

I found the school shut. A sign said:
EVACUATED TILL FURTHER NOTICE.

I had to catch my train. My employer was waiting.
Is she nice?

Very. So are the house and garden. But I was lonely without you.

One day when I was baking, Mrs. Davy asked, "Why are you sad?"

I told her everything. Mrs. Davy told me, "We'll find Mary Anne. What about her friend? Her parents will help us."

After that, it was easy! We found Bridget's father, he sent a cable to Canada, and the sadness was over.

Bridget has always brought me luck!

Mrs. Davy wants you to live with us. She likes children.

I'll be thirteen soon. I'm not a child.

You haven't changed. Still an answer for everything! If only *Vati* . . .
SIGH

Here is *Vati's* last postcard. It's only good-bye for now.

He writes, "I love you. Remember me."

War won't last forever.

ALL CHANGE!

OOOOOOO!
There's the all-clear, welcoming us to London.

• The End •

Dear Mutti and Vati

Glossary

Aros Welsh for "wait"

Aryan The name adopted by the Nazis to describe their idea of a "pure" German, who was considered to be fair-haired and blue-eyed.

Bach Welsh for "little," "small," or "dear"

Bara-menyn Welsh for "bread and butter"

Bore da Welsh for "good morning"

Concentration camp A place where people who did not fit the "Aryan" ideal were held without trial, subjected to slave labour and inhuman treatment—conditions that often led to death.

Dech y gwely Welsh for "come to bed"

Diolch Welsh for "thank you"

Diolch yn fawr Welsh for "thank you very much"

Gestapo The German political police force established by Adolf Hitler in 1933. They had far-reaching powers and were the most feared arm of the Nazi Party.

Hitler Adolf Hitler ruled Germany from 1933 to 1945. His tyrannical, cruel dictatorship ended after twelve years. When Hitler came to power, the traditional greeting of "Good day" was replaced, by law, with the compulsory "*Heil Hitler.*"

Ich heisse German for "my name is"

Kindertransport A rescue operation that began on December 1, 1938 and saved almost ten thousand children in Germany, Austria, and Czechoslovakia from the Nazis, before the outbreak of war on September 3, 1939 halted the mission.

Mairi Welsh for "Mary"

Mam Welsh for "mother"

Marks German currency

Marshall Göring Hermann Göring was the Commander of the German Air Force, and ranked second to Hitler in the Nazi party.

Mein Kampf German for *My Struggle*, the book that Hitler wrote in prison in 1924. Amongst many ideas, prominent were the plans he outlined for getting rid of the Jews.

Mochyn Welsh for "pig"

Mutti German for "mommy"

Nazis Members of the Nazi Party, who swore allegiance to Hitler. The Nazis under the leadership of their dictator, Hitler, occupied most of Europe. The end of the war in 1945 also brought an end to Hitler and his followers.

Nos da Welsh for "goodnight"

Oma German for "grandmother"

Opa German for "grandfather"

Refugee A person who flees his homeland to settle in another country because of persecution.

Shwmae Welsh for "hello"

Shwmae heno Welsh for "Hello. How are you?"

Sospan fach Welsh for "little saucepan"

Tŷ bach Welsh for "outhouse" or "privy"—literally, the "little house"

Vati German for "daddy"

Visa An official government document that permits entry to another country.

Y ferch Welch for "little girl"

. . . .

NOTE: In Welsh, every letter is pronounced.

Seeking Refuge is a work of fiction, set against the backdrop of events that surrounded the beginning of the Second World War (1939-1945). History is unalterable, and the facts are true, though Marianne's story is imaginary—one that children like her might have experienced.